Amanda
VISITS THE PLANETS

by Gina Ingoglia
illustrated by Maggie Smith

NEW YORK

Author's Note: In this book you will read that the planet Pluto is the farthest known planet from the Sun. However, beginning in 1979 Pluto entered a phase of its orbit that brings it closer to the Sun than Neptune. The two planets will return to their usual order in 1999.

Amanda Adams loved the library. Her mother was a librarian, so Amanda and her brother, Charlie, got to go there almost every day. One day Amanda decided to read a book about the planets.

"Listen to this Charlie," Amanda said. "'The Sun is a star.' That means it's a huge ball of glowing gas. It's just like the stars you see in the sky at night, only closer. But it's still not very close — it's more than 90 million miles from Earth."

"'Nine planets travel around the Sun,'" she continued. "'Each planet follows its own path, called an orbit. As the planets orbit, they also rotate' — that means they spin around like gigantic tops. 'The Sun and Earth and the other eight planets make up the solar system.'"

Amanda looked up from her book. "It would be great to visit the other planets, wouldn't it, Charlie?" she said. "Maybe I'd even take you with me. . . ."

The first four planets are called the "inner" planets. They are smaller than the next four planets and are made mostly of rock. The first planet, Mercury, is 36 million miles from the Sun. That means as it rotates, whichever side of the planet is facing the Sun gets very hot — more than 800 degrees. That's hot enough to melt a lead pipe. But the side that's facing away from the Sun is almost 300 degrees below zero!

Venus is the second planet from the Sun. It's often called Earth's "twin" because it's almost the same size as Earth.

Venus is hidden beneath a thick blanket of clouds. These clouds appear to be yellow because the light from the Sun reflects off them. That's why Venus glows so brightly when you see it in the sky.

Even though the clouds block a lot of the Sun's heat, Venus is still much too hot for people to live on. It's the hottest planet in the solar system.

Next comes our own planet, Earth. Scientists believe that Earth is the only planet in the whole solar system that can support life as we know it. It takes one year — 365 days — for Earth to orbit the Sun. While it's orbiting, Earth is also rotating, just like the other planets. It takes about 24 hours to make one complete rotation. It's daytime on the part of Earth that faces the Sun and it's nighttime on the part that faces away from it. That means that in the evening, when it starts to get dark, the part of Earth you're standing on is beginning to rotate away from the Sun.

The fourth planet is Mars. Some people think there are little green space creatures living on Mars. But Martians are only make-believe. If you went walking on Mars, all you would see is a lot of ice and dusty red rocks. There's also a long, deep crack on Mars, much larger than the Grand Canyon. This crack is so big that if it were on Earth, it would stretch all the way across the United States!

The next four planets are called the "outer" planets. Because they are very big and are made mostly of gases, they're known as the "gas giants."

Jupiter is the fifth planet from the Sun. It's the largest planet in the solar system. More than 1,300 planets the size of Earth could fit inside it.

There's a red spot on Jupiter that scientists believe is a never-ending storm of swirling gases. This storm is large enough to cover three Earths. Scientists call it the Great Red Spot.

The sixth planet from the Sun is named Saturn. It is very unusual-looking because it has beautiful bright rings spinning around it. The rings look smooth from a distance, but they're actually made of chunks of ice and billions of bits of rock and dust. These tiny pieces circle the planet, making it look as though Saturn is surrounded by solid rings.

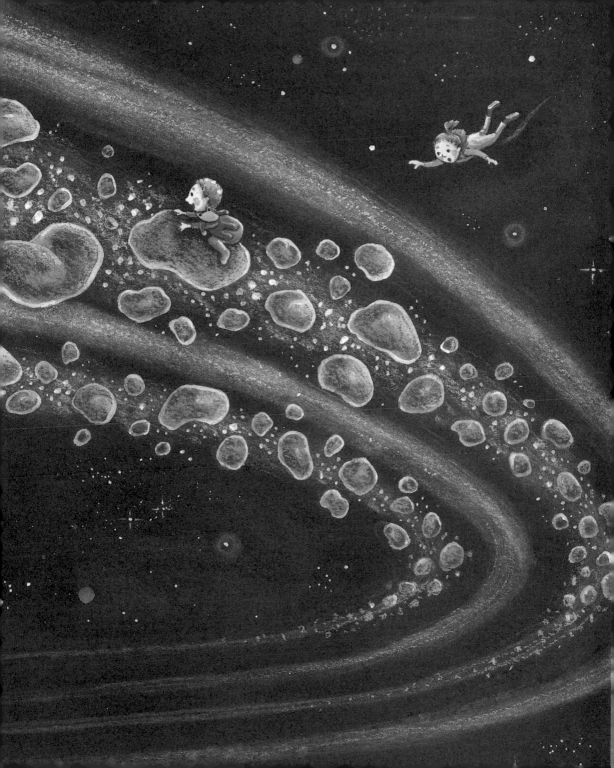

Next comes Uranus, the seventh planet. It looks bluish green in color and has faint rings around it. It's possible to see Uranus from Earth without a telescope if you wait for a dark, moonless night. But Uranus is so far away from Earth that all you'll be able to make out is a distant dot of light. It's so far from the Sun that the temperature on the planet is about 360 degrees below zero, and it takes 84 Earth-years to complete one orbit.

Uranus is the only planet that rotates on its side. As it orbits, one side faces the Sun for 42 years at a time. That means each half of the planet has daylight for 42 years while the other half is completely dark.

Neptune is the eighth planet from the Sun and the last of the gas giants. It is also somewhat bluish green in color, but even though it's much farther from the Sun than Uranus, it's not quite as cold because it generates its own heat. It's around 350 degrees below zero on Neptune. Like Jupiter, Neptune has a stormy spot, which scientists call the Great Dark Spot. This huge storm is equal in size to Earth.

Pluto is the ninth planet and the last one in our solar system. It's almost four billion miles from the Sun. If you could drive a car to Pluto it would take you 6,872 years to do it if you went 60 miles per hour the whole way. It takes more than 248 Earth-years for Pluto to complete one orbit.

Pluto is the smallest planet. It's even smaller than our moon. Some scientists think Pluto used to be one of Neptune's moons. Frozen gases cover the outside of the planet, but scientists think the inside is probably rock. It's so far from the Sun that there's hardly any light or heat.

"Amanda! Amanda!"

Amanda looked up from her book, blinking her eyes in surprise. "Oh, hi, Mom."

"Come on. It's time to go home," said her mother. "Where's Charlie?"

"The last I saw him was on Pluto," Amanda said.

"Pluto? What are you talking about?" Her mother looked around. "Oh, there he is." She picked Charlie up. "What were you reading today, Amanda?"

Amanda held up her book. "I was reading about the planets," she said. She smiled. "They're awfully interesting. I think when I grow up I'm going to be an astronaut!"